A Parents Magazine
Read Aloud Original.

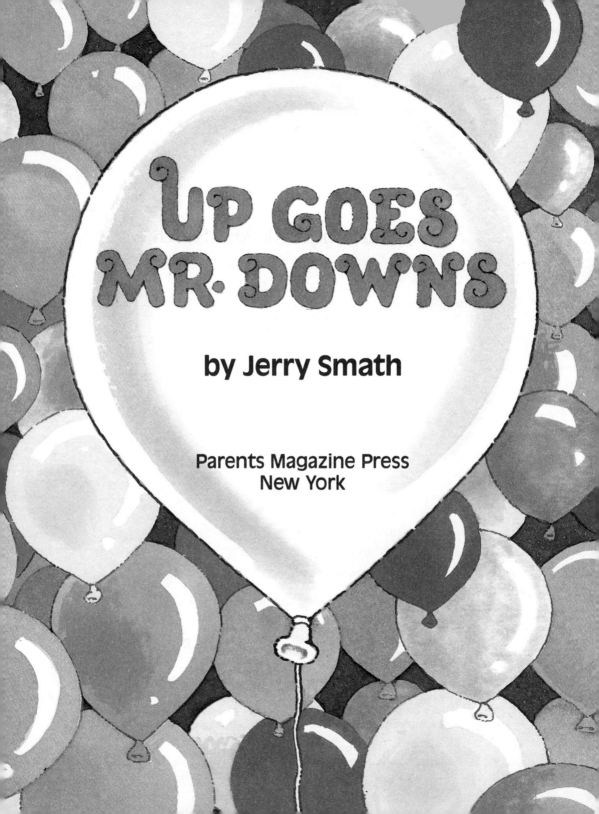

# Up Goes Mr. Downs

## by Jerry Smath

Parents Magazine Press
New York

To my wife, Valerie Kleckner Smath

Copyright © 1984 by Jerry Smath.
All rights reserved.
Printed in the United States of America.
10  9  8  7  6  5  4  3

Library of Congress Cataloging in Publication Data
Smath, Jerry.
Up goes Mr. Downs.
Summary: When his coat is inadvertently blown up with
a balloon hose, Mr. Downs floats up and away. Will he
ever come down?
1. Children's stories, American.   [1. Balloons—
Fiction]   I. Title.
PZ7.S6393Up  1984        [E]        84-1199
ISBN 0-8193-1137-5

Mr. and Mrs. Downs sold balloons.
Mr. Downs filled them while
Mrs. Downs called,
"Balloons for sale!"

One day, no one wanted balloons.
"Don't worry," said Mrs. Downs.
"Tomorrow is the big parade.
We will sell lots of balloons then."

They went home to rest
for the busy day ahead.

But that night, their new puppy,
Willy, barked at everything noisy.

"Hiss!" went the heater.
"Woof!" went Willy.

"Bong! Bong!" went the clock.
"Woof! Woof!" went Willy.

Mr. and Mrs. Downs
did not sleep at all.

"I'm so tired," said Mrs. Downs
the next morning.
"You stay home and rest,"
said Mr. Downs.
"I will sell balloons today.
And I will take Willy with me."

"Thank you, dear," said Mrs. Downs.
And she handed him the puppy.

On their way to town, Willy
barked at everything noisy.

"Honk!" went a bus.
"Woof!" went Willy.

"Vroom! Vroom!" went a scooter.
"Woof! Woof!" went Willy.

Before the parade started,
Mr. Downs filled his balloons.
Then he called, "Balloons for sale!"

But every time he filled a balloon,
Willy barked at the hissing hose.
"Hiss!" went the hose.
"Woof!" went Willy.

When Mr. Downs had sold almost
all his balloons,
he closed his eyes to rest.
Soon he fell fast asleep.

But the hose kept hissing.

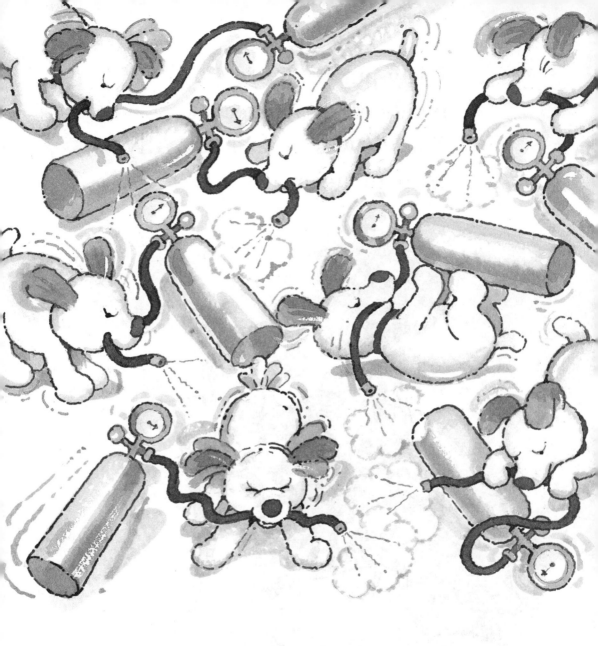

This time Willy didn't bark.
Instead, he tried to stop the noise.

Nothing worked until...

Willy put the hose
inside Mr. Downs' coat.
Then it was quiet and Willy
went to sleep, too.

While they were sleeping,
a very odd thing happened.
Mr. Downs' coat began to puff up
like a balloon.
It grew bigger and bigger.

Mr. Downs started to float away.
He woke up and called, "Help!"

Willy tried to pull him down.
But instead, they floated up together.
They went higher and higher.

Below them the parade was starting.

"Look at that funny balloon!"
called a boy.

"That's not a balloon,"
said his sister.
"That's Mr. Downs, the balloon man.
And he's calling for help!"

A policeman tried to catch him.
But Mr. Downs was floating too high.

A cowboy tried to lasso him.
But his lasso was too short.

"I'll get you down!"
called a fireman.
He was just about to grab him
when a big wind
carried Mr. Downs away.

The wind blew Mr. Downs
right toward home.
He saw Mrs. Downs asleep in bed.

"Wake up!" he called.
But Mrs. Downs did not hear him.
Just then, the clock started to bong.
"Woof! Woof!" barked Willy.

Mrs. Downs woke up.
Quickly, she opened the window
and pulled them both inside.

Mr. Downs floated up to the ceiling.
"Come down from there,"
called Mrs. Downs.
"I can't," Mr. Downs said.

"You need your rest," said Mrs. Downs.
"I'll help you take off your coat."

Whooosh!
Down came Mr. Downs.

As soon as they were in bed,
the heater began to hiss.
The clock began to bong...

But no one was listening.

## About the Author

**JERRY SMATH** has written and illustrated many books for children, including BUT NO ELEPHANTS and ELEPHANT GOES TO SCHOOL.

In UP GOES MR. DOWNS, the puppy named Willy is based on Mr. Smath's own dogs, Slipper and Sidney. "Luckily, they don't bark at night," says Mr. Smath. "But during the day they bark at everything, from squirrels in trees to the mailman coming down the road."

Mr. Smath and his wife, Valerie, a graphic designer, live in Westchester County, New York.